Greek Myths and Legends as Never Told Before

By the same author

THE COMIC STRIP ODYSSEY

Diane Redmond

Greek Myths and Legends as Never Told Before

Illustrated by Andrea Norton

VIKING

VIKING

Published by the Penguin Group
Penguin Books Ltd, 27 Wrights Lane, London W8 5TZ, England
Penguin Books USA Inc., 375 Hudson Street, New York, New York 10014, USA
Penguin Books Australia Ltd, Ringwood, Victoria, Australia
Penguin Books Canada Ltd, 10 Alcorn Avenue, Toronto, Ontario, Canada M4V 3B2
Penguin Books (NZ) Ltd, 182–190 Wairau Road, Auckland 10, New Zealand

Penguin Books Ltd, Registered Offices: Harmondsworth, Middlesex, England

First published 1993
1 3 5 7 9 10 8 6 4 2
First edition

Typeset by Datix International Limited, Bungay, Suffolk
Filmset in 16/17 Monophoto Palatino
Printed in England by Clays Ltd, St Ives plc

A CIP catalogue record for this book is available from the British Library

ISBN 0–670–84742–9

For Isabella, goddess of my hearth

The Greek Gods (the Immortals)

Zeus, the mightiest
of the Gods

Hera, his wife

Poseidon, the God
of the Sea and
brother of Zeus

Demeter, the
Goddess of the
Harvest and
sister of
Zeus

Athene, the
Goddess of Wisdor
and daughter of
Zeus

Hermes, the
Messenger God

Contents

1. Prometheus

The creator of man was an old God, the giant Prometheus. He took a lump of clay and shaped man, but he made him different from the other animals – he made him walk upright, on two feet, so that he could always look up to the sky and smile at the Gods. Zeus, mightiest of the Gods, breathed life into the clay and man was born.

Prometheus loved man and taught him everything he knew – how to build houses and make tools, how to read and write. He even told him the names of things and man learnt how to speak.

Zeus was furious.

'Great balls of fire, Prometheus!' he yelled. 'These mortal men will soon know more than me! Pack it in, right now!'

'God of Gods, please, let me give man one last thing?'

'What?' asked Zeus.

'Fire,' answered Prometheus.

'NO!!' thundered Zeus. 'You will teach him no more!'

He went off in a terrible huff, showering the earth with thunderbolts and rumbling the clouds in his temper. Prometheus was frightened until

Hermes popped up from behind a bush.

'Don't mind him,' said Hermes, the Messenger of the Gods. 'He's always in a bad mood with somebody.'

'I wish it wasn't me right now,' laughed Prometheus.

'He'll forget all about you, believe me,' said Hermes.

He was right too. Zeus did forget about Prometheus – at least for a while.

Prometheus watched man grow and longed to teach him more. He prayed to Pallas Athene, the Goddess of Wisdom.

'Goddess, please help me give man fire?'

'Thunder and lightning! Zeus will kill you,' cried Athene.

'If we're wise, Zeus will never know,' said clever Prometheus.

'All right,' agreed Athene. 'I'll lead you to Helios, the Sun God, he will give you fire.'

The next day she led Prometheus through secret passageways to the top of Mount Olympus, the sacred mountain of the Gods. There they waited for Helios, the Sun God. Every morning his chariot rises in the east and is pulled across the sky by golden horses with blazing tails. As Helios passes, carrying the sun behind him, the day begins. He gallops across the sky and then rides off into the west, taking the light with him. As soon as he's gone, dark night covers the earth.

As the day drew to a close, Prometheus could

hear the mighty sound of horses' hoofs pounding the air above Mount Olympus.

'Here he comes,' whispered Athene as Helios' sun chariot rolled overhead. Prometheus stepped forward and held out a dry fennel stalk. A spark from the chariot caught the tip of the stalk and Prometheus held fire in his hands.

'Goddess, thank you, thank you,' he cried.

'Hide it, before Zeus sees it,' whispered Athene.

Prometheus hid the tiny spark beneath his cloak and hurried down the mountain, back to the deep forests of Arcadia.

He waited a few days and then used the precious spark to light a fire. When man saw the flickering flames, he ran to Prometheus, terrified.

'Master, what is this magic?' he asked.

'Fire,' smiled Prometheus. 'The secret of life.'

He taught man how to make fire by rubbing dry sticks together, how to bake bread and meat, how to hammer hot bronze into swords and ploughs. It was indeed the most precious of his gifts, but man being foolish lit too many fires. Zeus, with his all-seeing eyes, saw the flames flickering on earth.

ZIP! ZIP! ZIP!

Thunderbolts fell from Olympia like rain.

'Prometheus! Why have you disobeyed me?'

Prometheus was terrified, but he answered truthfully. 'I wanted man to be better than the animals.'

'Why should man be better than the worms?' scoffed Zeus.

'Because I love him,' answered Prometheus.

'Fool! You'll fry in fire for this,' cried Zeus, and pointed a flaming thunderbolt straight at Prometheus.

'No, Father!' screamed Athene. 'Prometheus is an old God, you cannot kill him.'

Zeus knew his daughter was right. He laid down his thunderbolt and glared at Prometheus.

'If I cannot kill you, I will torture you, every day that you live.'

He chained Prometheus to a pillar in the Caucasian mountains, where greedy vultures pecked out his liver, day after day after day. Every night his liver grew again so that the vultures could feed on it the next day, and forever after. For thirty thousand years Prometheus was tortured, and all because he gave man fire – and what did man do with his great gift? He burnt the good earth and forgot the old God who had made him.

2. Pandora

Even though Prometheus suffered day after day, Zeus was still furious.

'I'll punish man for stealing my fire,' he raged. 'I'll make him a partner, a woman who will pester him to death.'

Pleased with his plan, Zeus took a lump of clay, shaped it into a woman and breathed life into it. Then he asked all the Gods and Goddesses to come along to see her.

'This is the first woman,' he said. 'I've made her to annoy man, so I want you all to give her gifts that will make her especially nasty.'

'I'll make her beautiful,' smiled Aphrodite.

'Beautiful! Why?' asked Zeus.

'So that she'll drive men mad with her pretty looks,' said Aphrodite.

'I'll make her cheeky,' laughed Hermes.

'I'll make her bad-tempered,' said Hera.

'I'll make her a liar,' said Hades.

Zeus laughed. 'Marvellous!' he cried. 'Pallas Athene, Goddess of Wisdom, what gift will you give woman?'

'Man has suffered enough,' said brave Athene. 'I'll teach the woman how to sew and cook.'

'Sew and cook!' laughed Hermes. 'That will

HELP man.'

'Somebody has to,' answered wise Athene. She looked at Zeus' creation, the first woman, with her silver hair and eyes the colour of the sea.

'What's her name?' she asked.

'Pandora,' said Zeus.

Zeus sent Pandora to live with Epimetheus, the brother of kind Prometheus.

'Here's a wedding present for you,' said Zeus, giving Epimetheus a golden box that sparkled with sapphires and diamonds.

'Thank you!' cried Epimetheus and immediately tried to open the box.

'It's locked,' said Zeus, 'and you must never, *ever* open it.'

Epimetheus was terribly disappointed, but nobody argued with Zeus.

'Here's the key which you must hide from Pandora – and remember, *never* open the box!'

From his throne on Mount Olympus, Zeus watched and chuckled as Epimetheus hid the box and the key.

'Idiot mortal, he's fallen for my trick. Now for some fun!'

Pandora was happy on earth, happy until the day she found the key to the box.

'What's this?' she asked.

'Oh, no!' cried Epimetheus. 'Have you opened Zeus' box?'

'What on earth are you talking about?' puzzled Pandora.

'Oh, nothing, nothing at all,' laughed Epimetheus, but Pandora knew he was lying.

She hid and watched Epimetheus put the key under a big stone jar.

'I'm going to get to the bottom of this business,' she said.

The next day while Epimetheus was out hunting, she sneaked the key from its hiding-place and searched the palace for the mystery box. It took her hours to find it, but when she did, she couldn't believe her eyes.

'Oh, it's beautiful!' she cried, and quickly put the key into the lock.

'Stop, Pandora!' whispered wise Athene. 'Think . . .'

Pandora glanced over her shoulder. 'Who's that?' she asked.

But nobody was there.

'Silly me! I'm hearing things,' she said.

Gently she lifted the lid of the box.

Shusha-shusha-shusha.

Something moved inside the box.

'What *is* it?' said Pandora as she threw back the lid.

W-H-O-O-O-O-S-H!

An enormous wind came rushing out of the box, the lid was blown sky-high and all the evils of the world poured out – sickness, poverty, pain, anger, jealousy and misery. They tumbled out and

were carried on the wind to the four corners of the world.

'Ha, ha, ha! That's blown it, Pandora!' laughed Zeus. 'Now you idiot mortals will suffer for stealing my fire — the whole lot of you, for ever and ever!'

But unknown to Zeus, wise Athene had slipped a small but precious gift into Pandora's box — it was the gift of hope. The Goddess saved us all, for without hope there is nothing.

3. Perseus and the Medusa

The King of Argos, Acrisius, had a daughter called Danaë who was very, very beautiful. Lots of brave heroes wanted to marry Danaë, but Acrisius had been told by the Gods that if Danaë were to marry and have a son, the child would grow up and kill him!

'Never!' shouted the King, and he locked his daughter in a tower so that nobody would see her – but Zeus had seen her.

Great balls of fire! thought Zeus, I must visit this wonderful mortal.

He left his cloud on Mount Olympus and hurried down to earth, but the guards wouldn't let him into Danaë's tower.

'Get out of it!' they yelled.

'How dare you – I'm ZEUS!'

'Oh, yeah?' laughed the guards. 'Tell us another.'

Zeus was just about to roast them with a blazing thunderbolt when he had a better idea.

'I'll trick them instead,' he smiled.

Disguised as a shower of golden rain, Zeus slipped through Danaë's prison window, right under the soldiers' noses.

'Funny,' puzzled the soldiers, as the shining rain

lit up Danaë's window. 'Never seen rain like this before.'

'Idiot mortals!' scoffed Zeus.

Danaë was even more beautiful than Zeus remembered. He stayed with her for as long as he could, then hurried back to Mount Olympus before his wife Hera found out where he'd been.

Several months later, Danaë gave birth to a strong, baby boy whom she called Perseus. When her father, King Acrisius, saw the baby he went M-A-D!

'You'll have to go, you can't stay here. Get out!'

'We can't go,' cried Danaë. 'Perseus is too young, he'll die.'

'Good, I hope he does!' shouted Acrisius. 'If he lives, I'll die.' He grabbed his sword and held it over the sleeping baby's head.

'No! No!' screamed Danaë. 'Kill me, not my baby!'

Acrisius hadn't the heart to kill either of them, so instead he put them in a wooden chest and pushed them out to sea. Dark waves crashed and smashed against the sides of the chest and Danaë was sure they would die.

'Zeus! Ruler of the skies, father of my son, save us!'

Zeus heard her prayers and guided the chest to the island of Seriphos, where it was washed ashore and found by a kind fisherman called Dictys.

'You can stay with me, I'll look after you,' he said.

Dictys was a good man. He brought Perseus up and taught him to fish and from an early age the boy showed a great talent for athletics. He could run like the wind and could throw the discus further than any other boy on the island. Everybody liked the golden-haired boy, everybody except Polydectes, the King of Seriphos. Polydectes wanted to marry Danaë, but she hated him.

'I'll make you rich, I'll make you happy – marry me,' said Polydectes.

'No! No! No!' cried Danaë.

It made Perseus very angry to see his mother frightened and upset by the wicked King.

'Leave her alone!' he shouted. 'You can't force her to marry you.'

Polydectes decided that it was time to get rid of pain-in-the-neck Perseus. With him out of the way, Danaë would soon marry him! He called Perseus to the palace and pretended to be his friend.

'There are some very nasty rumours going around Seriphos about you,' he said.

'Rumours! What rumours?' asked Perseus.

'People are saying that you're a softie — a mummy's boy!' said the King.

'Who?' shouted Perseus, clenching his fists. 'I'll show them who's a mummy's boy.'

'Calm down ... calm down,' said the King. 'I know it's not true, just gossip put about to upset you. Listen, I have a plan — do you want to hear it?'

Perseus nodded and the King smiled. Things were working out just as he'd hoped.

'I suggest you do something so brave that nobody will *ever* doubt your strength again,' he said.

'That's a brilliant idea,' agreed Perseus. 'What shall I do?'

'Kill the Medusa,' said the King.

Perseus went pale. The Medusa was the most deadly of the Gorgon monsters. With fangs like a wolf and talons like razors, it could tear a man apart in seconds.

'If you were to kill the Medusa and bring back its head, nobody would ever call you a mummy's boy again,' coaxed the evil King.

'Right, I'll do it,' said Perseus, and immediately set off to fight the Medusa.

His father, Zeus, knew that for all Perseus' strength and courage, he couldn't fight the monster

single-handed.

'Gods and Goddesses, protect my son!' he cried.

The Immortals rushed to help Perseus. Hermes tied wings to his sandals so that he could fly like a bird; Hades gave him a strong helmet to protect him in battle, but it was wise Athene who gave him the greatest gift.

'A shield!' cried Perseus, holding it before him and looking at his reflection in the shiny-bright metal.

'Not *just* a shield,' smiled Athene. 'It will save your life.'

'Huh?' said Perseus.

'When you reach the monster's den, *don't* look at the Medusa,' said Athene.

'Don't look!' laughed Perseus. 'How can I kill it if I don't look at it?'

'Look into the shield, it will reflect everything. Take care, Perseus, for if you should look at the Medusa, even a quick peek, you'll be turned to stone.'

Perseus thanked the kind Goddess and set off for the land of the Hyperboreans, a place in the far north where the sun rises and sets only once a year. With the wings on his sandals, Perseus flew across the world like a swallow. In the village near the Medusa's den, there were dozens of stone statues.

'Men, changed to stone by the Medusa,' said the terrified villagers.

'Where is this brute?' cried Perseus.

'Over th-th-there,' dithered the villagers.

To their astonishment, Perseus walked backwards to the den, checking in his shining shield for his first sight of the monster. Suddenly it loomed up – H-U-G-E!

'Sweet Athene, guide me now,' prayed Perseus.

The hideous thing scuttled towards him, a mountain of flesh with hissing snakes around its head.

Shaking in his boots, Perseus held his ground, waiting until the monster was right behind him. When he could feel its stinking, hot breath on his neck, he whirled round, his sword flashing in the sun.

'DIE!' he screamed.

Keeping his eyes firmly shut, he swept the air

around the Medusa and chopped its head clean off its shoulders.

'AHHHH!'

Even though its head was separated from its body, the monster kept on shrieking.

'A-H-H-H-H-H-H!!'

Then suddenly all was quiet. Perseus still didn't look at the monster, as Athene had warned him that even dead, the head of the Medusa could turn people to stone. Keeping his eyes tightly shut, he grabbed the snake-head and shoved it into a sack.

He flew back to Seriphos as fast as he could, but while he'd been away, King Polydectes had forced Danaë to marry him. When Perseus returned, his mother was dressed for the wedding.

'What are you doing?' he cried.

'Oh, Perseus, help me,' she sobbed. 'The King said he'd kill me if I didn't marry him.'

Then I will take him a wedding present,' smiled Perseus. 'One he will never forget . . .'

He found Polydectes in his palace, preparing the wedding feast. He couldn't believe his eyes when he saw Perseus striding towards him.

'You're back!' he gasped.

'Of course,' beamed Perseus. 'Here, I have a wedding gift for you.'

'For *me*?'

The last thing the King expected was a present from Perseus.

'Open it,' said Perseus. 'You've never seen anything like it before!'

As the King ripped open the sacking, Perseus glanced away. For a single second Polydectes looked into the Medusa's face and was then turned into a statue of solid stone.

With the King gone, Perseus lived happily on Seriphos. He became a famous athlete, the champion discus-thrower in Greece. One day he travelled to Argos to take part in the Olympic Games. Little did he know that his grandfather, Acrisius, was King of Argos, and how could Acrisius have guessed that the baby boy he tried to drown long ago had now grown into a great hero.

The games began. The packed stadium held its breath as Perseus picked up the discus. He breathed deeply and then spun round, but just as he was about to throw the discus, he fell. The discus zipped through the air, missing everybody in its path, and smashed into the King's head, killing him outright. King Acrisius had been slain by his grandson, the baby he'd tried to murder, but how could he have guessed that Perseus was the mighty son of Zeus?

4. Persephone

Demeter is Goddess of the Harvest, the sister of Zeus, but altogether a gentler, kinder Goddess. She feeds the earth with soft rain and sunshine, she makes the flowers bloom and gives us wheat and corn at harvest time. When the earth was young, there was no autumn or winter, just springtime and summer. The earth was always beautiful, with flowers and fruit growing all the year round — it was like paradise.

Demeter lived in Sicily with her lovely daughter, Persephone. They were happy on their island until one day Hades spotted Persephone gathering flowers in the meadows near Mount Etna.

Hades was God of the Underworld, the land of the dead. He hardly ever left his dark kingdom, but one day the volcano, Etna, erupted. It cracked the earth and streams of boiling-hot lava poured down the mountainside.

BOOM! BOOM! BOOM! went the exploding volcano.

'Hell-fire! What is that noise?' cried Hades.

He called for his chariot, which was pulled by four black stallions with flying manes and flashing eyes. Crack! went his whip across their backs. The horses reared up and galloped through the halls of hell.

With pounding hoofs and flying tails, they jumped the River Styx and raced up to earth, bursting through a crack in the surface near Etna. Dazzled by the bright sunshine, Hades drew in his chariot and covered his eyes. When he opened them, Persephone was standing before him with her arms full of flowers.

'It is the Goddess Aphrodite,' he whispered.

'No,' laughed Persephone, 'I am the daughter of Demeter. My name is Persephone.'

'You are the most wonderful thing I have ever seen,' he cried, and before she could say another word, he'd grabbed hold of her and pushed her into his chariot.

'Go! Go! Go!' he yelled at his horses, lashing his whip across their sweating backs. Neighing in fear, the horses turned around and galloped back to Hades.

'M-O-T-H-E-R!!' screamed Persephone, but the earth had closed up behind her – she was a prisoner in hell.

Hades led her to his dark palace, which was draped in black silk and lit with gloomy oil lamps. Ghosts came in, carrying trays of food and wine.

'Eat,' smiled Hades. 'Welcome to my kingdom. You will be my queen.'

'No! No! No!' screamed Persephone. 'I want to go home, I want my mother – NO!'

She cried for days and weeks and months, but Hades wouldn't let her leave the underworld.

'She is the light of my life, I will keep her for ever,' he told his brother Zeus.

Meanwhile poor Demeter was going mad. She had searched the island from top to bottom, but couldn't find her daughter anywhere.

'I will not rest until I find my Persephone,' she wept.

She travelled the world, asking everybody, 'Have you seen my daughter?'

Nobody had seen her, nobody could tell her anything. For a year she journeyed north, south, east and west, then she went back home to Sicily. Her heart was broken. She no longer cared about the flowers and the harvest and she hated the beauty of the earth, which reminded her of Persephone.

'I will curse it,' she cried.

Flowers died, the trees lost their beautiful leaves. Ripe fruit rotted on the branch and rain fell from

the sky. 'What is this wet stuff?' asked the people of the world.

Cold winds froze the earth and snow lay in deep drifts for months. Winter came for the first time and there was no food for the children.

'What shall we do?' cried the people of the earth. 'Demeter has forgotten us.'

'Zeus, help us.'

Zeus yawned and peeled a grape. 'These mortals are always moaning,' he grumbled.

'Father,' cried Athene, 'you must help them or they'll die.'

'I can't take Persephone from Hades,' answered Zeus. 'He's the God of the Underworld — and powerful too.'

'You are the God of Gods,' said clever Athene. 'You can do *anything* you want!'

'Great balls of fire, you're the Goddess of Wisdom, *you* do something for a change!' snapped Zeus and went off in a thunderstorm tantrum.

Poor Demeter had given up all hope of ever finding her daughter. One day she lay by a stream and wept and wept. The spirit of the water cried out to her, 'Demeter, Demeter, weep no more. I can tell you where Persephone is.'

'Ah!' gasped Demeter. 'Where?'

'In Hades,' answered the river.

'Hades! Is she dead?'

'No,' answered the river. 'The God of the Underworld has married your daughter and made her his queen.'

'Are you sure?'

'I saw her with my own eyes as I passed through the underworld,' answered the river.

'Thank you, oh, thank you!' cried Demeter.

She jumped into her chariot and drove to Mount Olympus.

'Brother Zeus! Where are you?' she called.

'What is it, sister?' he asked.

'Our brother Hades has stolen my daughter.'

'So?' snapped Zeus.

'I must have her back immediately,' cried Demeter.

Now the truth was that Zeus did not want to upset his brother. It was easier all round if Persephone stayed in Hades, but he could see that

Demeter was in no mood for doing him favours.

'I warn you,' said Demeter. 'If Persephone is not given back to me, I will blast the earth with wind and ice and destroy all its people.'

Zeus shrugged. He didn't care about the mortals — they were even more of a headache than his pain-in-the-neck sister.

'Father, you *must* do something!' begged Athene.

'Thunder and lightning!' bellowed Zeus. 'Will you stop nagging me?'

The Goddesses glared at him, fury blazing in their eyes. Zeus knew that if they joined power, they could boil him in oil and eat him for breakfast.

'All right, all right. Persephone can come back,' he said, 'as long as she hasn't eaten any food during her stay in the underworld.'

Demeter smiled, 'Thank you, brother.'

Zeus sent Hermes the Messenger down to the underworld.

'You must release Persephone,' said Hermes.

'Who said?' roared Hades.

'Your brother Zeus,' said Hermes.

'Hell-fire! Tell him to mind his Olympian business!'

'He is the God of Gods, he must be obeyed,' Hermes told him. 'Zeus says, as long as Persephone has not eaten any food in the underworld, she can go back to earth.'

'I have eaten nothing!' cried Persephone.

'Liar!' shouted Hades. 'I saw you eat seven pomegranate seeds.'

'Now there'll be trouble!' moaned Hermes.

There was too, a lot of it. Hermes the Messenger was dizzy going up to Olympus and down to Hades. Finally they all agreed that Persephone could go back home *but*, because she'd eaten the food of the dead, she could only stay half the year on earth and not the whole year.

Laughing with joy, Persephone returned home to her mother. For six months she lived with her in the sunny meadows of Sicily. Flowers sprang up wherever they walked, birdsong filled the air, green leaves grew on the trees and the corn ripened in the fields. Persephone had come home, the harvest would be great and the earth would grow beautiful again. After the corn had been cut, Hades appeared in his black chariot and took Persephone away. As the earth's surface closed over her head, the halls of hell echoed with Persephone's tears. Demeter wept too, along with the people as the earth grew cold and bare.

'She'll come back to us,' the mortals told each other – and she always does. In the springtime of the year, when life begins again.

5. Jason and the Golden Fleece

It was Hermes, the Messenger God, who created the giant ram with a long fleece of shimmering gold. He sent the ram to save two children, a boy called Phrixus and a girl called Helle. They lived with their father, who loved them deeply, but their stepmother hated them. She made up her mind to have the little children killed, but Hermes took pity on them and sent the giant ram to rescue them. The ram flew over the Greek islands, and when he saw the two children playing on a beach, he landed beside them and said, 'Quickly, climb on to my back.'

The children were delighted. They jumped up and rolled over and over in his soft, silky fleece.

'Hold on tight,' called the ram, and with a leap took off and flew through the air.

Laughing and giggling with excitement, the children held on to the ram, the boy to his huge curling horns, the girl to his fleece, but as they passed over the sea, Helle let go.

'Look, Phrixus,' she cried, and pointed to the sea far below. 'Look how beautiful it is.'

Suddenly the ram turned direction and Helle fell, tumbling down, down, down through the blue sky into the crashing sea where she drowned. To this day that stretch of water in Asia is called the Hellespont, in memory of the little girl who died there so long ago.

The ram flew on and on, with Phrixus weeping for his sister, but not daring to look back in case he fell too. They finally stopped in Colchis. Phrixus was relieved but sad too, as he'd lost his sister and he knew he had to kill the golden ram. Zeus would expect a sacrifice, a thank you gift for his safe journey. If he didn't get it, there'd be big trouble!

Phrixus quickly killed the ram, offering the blood and bones to the Gods, but he kept the shimmering golden fleece and hung it on a huge tree. The King of the island, Aëtes, was delighted with the fleece.

'I'll take care of it,' he promised and he did, for a very long time.

Far away another boy was growing up. His name was Jason and he was King of Iolcos, but his wicked uncle, Pelias, had taken his throne when he was a baby and sent Jason away. He grew up in the mountains, with his teacher, Chiron, who was half man, half horse. Chiron taught Jason many things, like how to shoot an arrow faster and further than any other boy, and how to run and wrestle like a grown man. Jason could play sweet music and recite poetry too.

'You're lucky,' said Chiron proudly. 'Everybody loves you.'

When Jason had grown into a young man, Chiron said, 'It's time to leave the mountains and go back to Iolcos. The throne belongs to you and you must take it from your uncle, Pelias.'

Jason was sad to leave but excited too. He wanted adventures, great adventures that would make him famous for all time.

When he got to the city of Iolcos, Jason went straight to the King, his wicked uncle, Pelias.

'I am Jason, this land belongs to me!'

'Indeed?' said the King. 'Prove it!'

'I'll bring back the Golden Fleece,' cried Jason. 'Is that enough proof?'

The people gasped but the wicked King just smiled. The boy was a bigger fool than he had thought. Steal the Golden Fleece? No chance! Young Jason would be dead before the year was out – but that was fine by Pelias.

'May the Gods sail with you, Jason,' said the King.

And in a funny sort of way, they did!

The man who built Jason's huge sailing ship was called Argos, he called the ship *Argo* and the crew who sailed in her became known as the Argonauts. Jason took the bravest heroes in the land – fifty-three men and one woman, Atalanta, who was the most skilful archer in the world. He also took Orpheus, the greatest musician ever known, Herakles, the strongest man in the world, Castor and Pollux, the twin sons of Zeus, and Lynceus, whose eyes were so sharp, he could see straight through the earth to the other side.

After weeks and weeks of preparation, they set sail across the wide blue sea. With the wind in their sails, they made good progress until they came to the Clashing Rocks. These huge rocks floated on the waves, moving in and out, trapping and squashing whatever came between them. Lynceus spotted them first.

'The Clashing Rocks!' he yelled from his look-out.

Jason had been warned of the rocks and knew exactly what to do.

'Drop the sail,' he yelled to the crew. 'Prepare to row for your lives.'

The Argonauts waited at their oars and watched Jason take a white pigeon from a basket. He threw it up into the air and the bird headed straight for the rocks.

'Watch out!' called Castor. 'You'll get flattened.'

The crew held their breath as the rocks closed together, making the waves thunder, but the bird flew right through and safely out the other side.

'It's a sign from the Gods,' smiled Jason. 'They'll allow us to pass through unharmed.'

'Heave!' shouted Herakles. Pushing on the oars with all their might, the crew rowed the ship between the huge, shuddering rocks. The waves sent them spinning and whizzing, but they made it through.

'The Gods be praised,' sighed Pollux.

'Raise the sail,' called Jason, and with the wind behind them, they skipped across the foaming sea, happy to leave the Clashing Rocks behind them.

At long last they came to Colchis on the Black Sea.

'Drop anchor!' called Jason. 'I must speak to the King of this land.'

Aëtes, who was still King of Colchis, became very angry when Jason told him he wanted the Golden Fleece.

'You've got a cheek!' he stormed. 'First prove you're man enough to have it.'

Jason sighed — why did these silly kings keep making his life so difficult?

'What do you want me to do?' he asked.

'Catch my fire-breathing bulls, fasten them to a plough and plant a field with dragons' teeth.'

'Is that *all*?' laughed Jason.

Now Aëtes had a daughter, Medea the evil witch, who had fallen in love with Jason and didn't want to see him die.

'In exchange for a kiss, I will tell you all you need to know to save your life,' she whispered.

Jason immediately kissed her. Medea smiled.

'Listen carefully, hero. The night before you face the bulls, you must eat wild crocus from the mountains. Their magic will protect you.'

That night Jason did as Medea had told him, and the next day he went out to catch the bulls. A big crowd had gathered and they couldn't believe their eyes when they saw Jason walk straight up to the bulls.

'He'll be burnt to cinders!' they gasped.

Fire blazed from the bulls' nostrils, but Jason walked right through it without getting so much as a blister. He harnessed the bulls to the plough and planted the dragons' teeth in the King's field. No sooner were the teeth planted when they popped up again, as an army of soldiers who raised their swords and marched on Jason.

'Hah!' cried the crowd. 'This time he's mincemeat!'

Jason didn't bat an eyelid. He calmly picked up a boulder and threw it into the middle of the field. It hit a soldier, who turned round and stabbed the man next to him. Suddenly all the soldiers began to fight, clashing swords and stabbing each other, until every one of them lay dead and the ploughed field ran with their blood. The crowd began to chant and clap.

'GIVE HIM THE FLEECE! GIVE HIM THE FLEECE!'

King Aëtes was furious, but he couldn't refuse the crowd what they wanted.

'The fleece is yours,' he snapped. 'Take it.'

The King never mentioned the dragon-serpent that protected the fleece – but Medea did.

'You must take Orpheus with you,' she said.

'Orpheus!' laughed Jason. 'He can only sing.'

'His song will save your life,' she promised.

*

When night fell, Medea led Jason and Orpheus to the tree where the Golden Fleece hung. It shimmered in the moonlight, lighting up the dragon-serpent curling and hissing beneath it.

'S-s-s-s-s-s-s.'

'Tell Orpheus to sing,' whispered Medea.

'Sing! At a time like this,' cried Jason.

'Sing, hero — or die!' said Medea.

Orpheus played his lute and sang a song so beautiful, the night seemed to stand still. Sweet music filled the air and drifted away into the dark, starry sky. Jason was entranced until Medea gave him a poke in the ribs.

'Move!' she snapped. 'Orpheus has charmed the dragon-serpent with his heavenly voice.'

The dragon-serpent was snoozing with a dozy smile on its face.

'Grab the fleece!' cried Medea.

Jason jumped over the sleeping monster and pulled the fleece from the tree-top.

'Run for your life!' shouted Medea.

The three of them raced through the dark forest, praying with every breath that the dragon-serpent would not wake and chase them. They reached the harbour and quickly jumped aboard the *Argo*.

'Set sail!' yelled Jason. 'The fleece is ours.'

'HURRAY!' cheered the Argonauts, and catching the night breeze in their sails, they shot out of the harbour and zipped across the open sea.

As rosy dawn lit the sky, Lynceus spotted a ship on the skyline.

'My father!' cried Medea, who had escaped with Jason, bringing her little brother along too.

'R-O-W!' bellowed Jason.

The Argonauts grabbed the oars and heaved with all their might, but no matter how hard they rowed, King Aëtes' ship came nearer . . . and nearer . . . and nearer.

'The Gods save us,' prayed Jason, as the ships were almost neck and neck.

'I'll save you!' cried Medea, and grabbing hold of her little brother, she slit his throat from ear to ear.

'NO!' screamed Jason, but it was too late. The

boy slumped on to the deck and Medea started to chop him up into little pieces.

'Food for the fishes,' she smiled, as she tossed pieces of the boy's body into the sea. 'This should stop my father in his tracks.'

It certainly did stop the King. When he saw his son's body floating on the waves towards him, he stopped his ship and headed home, heartbroken. Jason and the Argonauts sailed on, but Jason was disgusted by the witch Medea. The first island they came to, he stopped the *Argo* and threw her off.

'Good riddance to bad rubbish!' called the Argonauts.

'You won't get rid of me!' screamed Medea.

But they did! They left her cursing them to Hades and sailed home with the Golden Fleece.

'Now make me King!' said Jason.

Pelias couldn't argue with his nephew any more. Jason became King of Iolcos and all his boyhood dreams had come true. He was a great Greek hero and would be famous for all time – Jason the fearless leader of the mighty Argonauts!

6. The Labours of Herakles

Herakles was the strongest and the mightiest of all the Greek heroes.

His mother was mortal, another beautiful woman whom Zeus fell madly in love with. When Hera, Zeus' wife, heard about his new girlfriend she was furious.

'I am sick and tired of your hanky-panky!' she yelled. 'How dare you go off with a mortal woman and never give a thought to me. I'm your wife — and a great Goddess at that!'

Zeus growled bad-temperedly and whizzed a few thunderbolts across the sky.

'Great balls of fire!' he snapped. 'Stop nagging me or I'll send you to Hades for a fortnight!'

'Hah!' scoffed Hera. 'Try it and I'll tie *you* in knots for a fortnight.'

Zeus shut up fast. Hera had tied him in knots a couple of centuries earlier and he hadn't liked it a bit.

'I'll tell you something, if this mortal woman has a baby — your baby — I'll strangle it, in its cradle!'

The mortal woman did have a baby, Zeus' son, and Hera hit the Olympian roof.

'Die, brat!' she screamed, and threw two

poisonous snakes into the cradle, but the baby was Herakles, the strongest man that ever lived. Even though he was only a few days old, he grabbed the wriggling snakes in his little fat fists and strangled them. Hera couldn't believe her eyes.

This is some mortal! she thought to herself and decided to let the baby live — at least for a bit longer.

Every year that passed, Herakles grew bigger, stronger and more powerful. The finest athletes in Greece taught him to run and wrestle, and famous warriors taught him to throw the javelin and fight with clubs and swords.

'He's extraordinary,' they all said. 'Superman — a phenomenon!'

Because he knew he'd been blessed by the Gods, Herakles wanted to use his strength to help people. He went to visit the Oracle at Delphi and there the wise man spoke to him.

'You must do good,' said a strange, whispering voice.

'How?' asked Herakles.

'Go to Mycenae and live with King Eurystheus. He will tell you what to do.'

And that's how the labours of Herakles really began.

'Your first labour,' said King Eurystheus, 'is to kill the Lion of Nemea. To prove you've killed it, take the skin off its back, and bring it here to me.'

Killing a lion was no problem for a strong man like Herakles.

'This is no ordinary lion,' warned the King. 'No weapon, so far, has ever been sharp enough to cut its skin.'

'I'll think of something,' said Herakles, and set off with his spear, sword, club and a thick rope net.

He reached Nemea after many days travelling and asked the locals where the famous man-eating lion lived.

'L-l-l-lion!' they cried. 'You can't go near that. It's eaten four babies and a donkey this week.'

'Somebody's got to kill it,' said Herakles.

The locals nodded; they didn't mind who killed it – as long as it wasn't them.

'The lion lives over there,' they said. 'In a den knee-deep in bones and skin.'

'Thanks,' said Herakles. 'See you later.'

'You'll be lucky,' whispered the locals, and ran home and hid under their beds.

As Herakles walked up the hills, he tripped over bones of all sizes – big bones, little bones, shin bones, back bones, even head bones! He didn't have to look far for the cave – he could smell it a mile away.

Meanwhile the Nemean Lion could smell Herakles. 'Yum, yum! Man for supper,' he slurped, and went out to meet him.

Herakles couldn't believe the size of the lion – it was huge! As big as a horse, with a flaming mane and eyes that blazed fire. If he hadn't been such a hero, he would have turned tail and run for his life, but instead he grabbed his spear and took aim. The lion sprang forwards and Herakles hurled the spear straight at him. Z-I-P!! The spear hit the lion, but instead of cutting into its skin, the arrowhead shattered and the spear bounced into the bushes. The lion tossed his mane and snarled.

'You don't frighten me, Goldilocks!' laughed Herakles, and pulling out his sword he charged on the lion. Herakles stabbed the sword into the lion's chest, but to his astonishment nothing happened. The skin didn't bleed, break or even scratch. Instead the sword split clean in two and Herakles was left with only his club.

'This time you're supper!' howled the lion.

He opened his enormous mouth, his fangs sharp as razors, and Herakles whacked the club SMACK! in the lion's mouth.

'Oooh, that hurt,' said the lion and stomped off into his den.

'Hurt?' cried Herakles. 'A bash like that should have knocked his socks off! I need more strength to kill this monster; I need wisdom too.' He fell to his knees and prayed to Pallas Athene, Goddess of Wisdom. 'Sweet Goddess, guide me, tell me what to do.'

Athene heard his prayers and answered them.

'Brave Herakles, take your net and cover the lion's cave, then creep inside and kill the beast with your bare hands.'

Herakles gulped. That's a tall order! he thought, but he did just as Athene had told him.

He fixed his net across the den, crept in through another entry and tracked the Nemean Lion through the dark, stinking passageways. Herakles finally cornered the lion. The lion snarled.

'GRRRRR!' Herakles wasn't scared. He grabbed the lion by the throat, pressing his fingers tighter and tighter. The lion scratched and clawed, but Herakles kept on squeezing and squeezing until every bit of breath had left the lion's body. Finally it was still – dead still.

'Now to get the skin off its back,' said Herakles, but how when there wasn't a weapon sharp enough to cut through its skin?'

Again Athene, Goddess of Wisdom, helped him.

'Use the lion's claw,' she whispered.

'Thank you, Goddess!' prayed Herakles and chopped off one of the lion's huge claws.

It cut through the skin like butter. Wrapping the lion's skin round his body, Herakles returned to Mycenae, very pleased with himself, but King Eurystheus didn't spend too long congratulating him.

'Off you go on your second labour and take that stinking Nemean Lion's skin with you!' he said. 'This time I want you to kill the Hydra.'

Brave Herakles didn't bat an eyelid. He set off for the coastland near Argos where Hydra, the nine-headed monster, lived. Luckily he took his wise servant, Iolaus, with him, otherwise he might never have come back. Among the trees by the sea they heard the loud hissing and gurgling of the Hydra.

'Master, watch out!' warned Iolaus.

Suddenly the monster was on them, its nine tongues spitting, its nine eyes blazing.

'DIE!!' screamed Herakles and with all his strength he struck the Hydra and whacked off one of its heads.

One down, eight to go, thought Herakles – no such luck!

'Watch out!' screamed Iolaus.

The minute the dead head had touched the ground, another one had grown. Taking a deep breath, Herakles ran at the Hydra. He chopped off three heads in as many seconds, but they all grew

back immediately, like flowers popping up in the springtime.

'Ha, ha, ha!' laughed Hera from Mount Olympus. 'I've waited a long time to see you die, Herakles. Now I'll make it even more painful for you.'

At Hera's command, two giant crabs with claws as big as JCBs came scuttling across the sand and grabbed Herakles by the ankles.

This is a tight spot! thought Herakles, and taking up his club, he smashed each of the crabs on the head. His strength was so great that the crabs' skulls popped wide open and their brains fell out.

'Master!' cried Iolaus, who'd been watching the

fight from the top of a tree. 'I've had a brainwave.'

'Good! I'm right out of clever ideas,' joked Herakles.

'You chop off the Hydra's heads and I'll singe the ends with a burning log,' called Iolaus.

'How come I get all the good bits?' laughed Herakles.

He faced the Hydra with Iolaus behind him, shaking like a leaf as he held on to his burning torch.

ZAP! ZAP! ZAP! ZAP! went Herakles' sword. Heads fell in all directions, but before they could grow again, Iolaus singed each bleeding stump with his red-hot torch. Finally there was only one head left. Herakles clubbed it to jelly and then buried it in the sand.

He took the Hydra's body back to Mycenae, but King Eurystheus was not pleased.

'Must you bring that smelly monster in here?' grumbled the King.

'I thought you might like to see it,' said Herakles.

'Not at all!' snapped the King. 'It's put me right off my dinner and, anyway, hero, you cheated!!'

'CHEATED!' gasped Herakles.

'You shouldn't have let your servant help you,' said the King. 'That wasn't part of the deal.'

'By the Pillars of Herakles, if he hadn't helped me, I wouldn't be here to tell the tale!'

'Your next task will be even harder,' said King **Eurystheus.**

'That'll make a nice change!' sighed Herakles.

'You must clean out the stables of King Augeas – in a day!'

Herakles gulped. King Augeas lived in Elis, *another* marathon journey to the ends of the earth. He owned a thousand cattle which were kept in huge stables that had never, *ever* been cleaned out and were two metres deep in dung. The air stank, the island stank, the people stank – and so did King Augeas!

'The filth from the stables is causing sickness and disease,' said Eurystheus. 'It's up to you to clean them, Herakles.'

'Thanks!' laughed Herakles. 'Have you got a peg I could borrow for my nose?'

It took nearly a year to reach Elis, but Herakles had his servant, Iolaus, to keep him company on the way. King Augeas was delighted to see them both and was thrilled by Herakles' offer.

'I've come to clean out your stables – in a day,' he said.

'Unless your day has a thousand hours, you'll never do it,' laughed Augeas. 'The muck's two metres high.'

'I know,' sniffed Herakles. 'I can smell it from here.'

'Bit pongy, isn't it?' agreed Augeas, who was far too lazy to clean up the stables himself. 'Well, off you go, don't let me hold you up.'

'If I manage the job, will you give me a piece of the land I clear?' asked Herakles.

'Certainly,' agreed Augeas. 'Take whatever you want.'

Herakles and Iolaus set off for the stables, behind which ran two huge rivers.

'I think you've bitten off more than you can chew here,' moaned Iolaus.

'Watch me,' smiled Herakles. 'I have a plan.'

Lifting boulders as big as trains, he blocked both rivers and directed them straight towards the stables of Augeas.

'This'll shift that mountain of muck,' he said.

Standing on a high cliff, he and Iolaus watched the teeming waters of the rivers join together and thunder downhill. They rushed through the filthy

stables, sweeping away the dung that had been piling up for twenty years. W-H-O-O-S-H!! it went, straight out to sea.

King Augeas inspected his sparkling-clean stables and readily agreed that Herakles had done a marvellous job.

'Take your land, hero,' he said, 'and welcome.'

Herakles chose a fine stretch of land which has been used, by the Greeks, from that day to this for the site of their Olympic Games. When he returned to Mycenae, King Eurystheus was ready and waiting for the next task.

'Your fourth labour is to capture the fire-breathing Cretan Bull,' he said.

Herakles yawned. 'I've been round the world twice and just mucked out a stable two metres deep in dung! Do you think I could just stop off for a bite and a wash?' he asked.

'This isn't a holiday, you nincompoop!' said the King. 'This is hard work.'

'I've noticed,' said Herakles.

'No more complaining,' warned the King. 'Or I shall have a few words to say to Zeus about you.'

'Sorry,' said Herakles, who knew that even a hero has to keep his mouth shut sometimes.

'Now off you go, on your fourth labour.'

Luckily Crete wasn't too far away and Herakles, with Iolaus, went straight to the city of Knossos and spoke to King Minos.

'We've come to capture the Cretan Bull,' said Herakles.

'You'll be lucky!' cried Minos, who was so terrified of the bull, he hadn't been out of his palace for years.

'We'll see,' answered Herakles calmly. 'Where does it live?'

'Outside the city walls.'

'At least this beast has no magical powers,' said Iolaus as they walked around the city walls, looking for the bull.

'That's a relief,' said Herakles, but when he saw the size of the bull, his heart sank into his boots.

'What a whopper!' gulped Iolaus.

The beast threw back its head and breathed flames ten metres long. It pounded the ground with its huge hoofs, then let out a bellow that turned their blood to water. As the bull charged, Herakles leapt sideways and sprang on to its back. Grabbing hold of its razor-tipped horns, he wrestled the bull to the ground where Iolaus quickly tied it up.

'Let's see what King Eurystheus has to say about this,' said Herakles, lifting the huge bull on to his shoulders.

'Get rid of it!' screamed Eurystheus when he saw the bull, alive and kicking, on Herakles' back.

'Great Zeus! I can't do anything to please you,' said Herakles.

'Just stop bringing monsters into my palace!' dithered the King, and hid in a cupboard until Herakles had set the bull free.

The fifth labour took Herakles to the far north, to the land of Thrace, ruled over by the warrior King, Diomedes. He was a great fighter, with a war chariot that was pulled by four flesh-eating mares, who were fed enemy soldiers for breakfast, lunch and supper.

'What do these horses eat when Diomedes runs out of enemies?' asked Iolaus.

'Anybody Diomedes can get his hands on,' answered Herakles.

Neither of them fancied staying in the palace of Diomedes, as they were worried he might serve them up for dinner. They headed straight for the stables where they found the mares tied up. When they saw the strangers, they rattled their chains and snapped their teeth.

Herakles smashed their chains with his club. The mares reared up on their hind legs and galloped out into the yard. The guards came running, but the mares kicked them to death, then ate them! Still hungry, they jumped the palace walls and trotted into Diomedes' bedroom where they ate him too!

Once they'd eaten their master, they became tame and very friendly. Herakles led them back proudly to Mycenae.

'Ahhhh!' screamed King Eurystheus. 'I didn't say capture the blooming mares, I said kill them!'

'But they're nice now,' explained Herakles. 'Look, they're really friendly.'

He gave the horses sugar lumps and they licked his hands for more.

'Get them out!' yelled the King, and jumped into the cupboard *again.*

Herakles set them free.

'Neigh!' they called to him, then galloped off into the mountains of Arcadia.

After King Eurystheus had got over his shock, he set Herakles his *sixth* labour.

'What more?' cried Herakles. 'Your Majesty, when will I get a rest?'

'After twelve years of working for me you can rest all you want,' answered the King. 'For your sixth labour, I want you to go to Mount Atlas and

bring back the Golden Apples of the Hesperides.
Atlas will tell you where to find them, he's been
there for centuries.'

'Looks like I'll be gone a long time,' sighed
Herakles.

'Years, with a bit of luck,' snapped the King,
who was sick of Herakles and his horrible monsters. 'Now go away and *please* don't hurry back!'

A year later Herakles and Iolaus arrived at Mount
Atlas in Africa where poor Atlas stood, holding up
the world.

'Ah! It's a hard job,' groaned Atlas. 'My back's killing me!'

'Do you know where I can find the Golden Apples of the Hesperides?' asked Herakles.

'Certainly, my daughters guard them,' answered Atlas.

'Do you think they would let me have some?' asked Herakles.

'Yes, but I would have to ask them myself,' said Atlas.

'How?' asked Herakles.

'Well . . . if you would be so kind as to hold up the world, I could nip down the hill and speak to them,' said Atlas.

'All right,' said Herakles.

Atlas lifted the world off his big shoulders and stretched. 'Ah! That's wonderful!' he sighed, and smiled up at the sun for the first time in twenty years.

'Don't be long,' said Herakles.

'I'll be back just as soon as I can,' promised Atlas, but he was gone a long time and the weight of the world pushed down, heavier and heavier, on to Herakles' aching shoulders. What if he doesn't come back? thought Herakles. I'll be stuck here for ever and ever and ever, with this terrible load on my shoulders.

Suddenly, when Herakles thought he couldn't stand it a minute longer, Atlas came running up the hill with his arms full of Golden Apples.

'Sorry I was so long, Herakles, but it was wonderful to be free again. Wonderful!'

Sighing sadly, he bent over and Herakles put the world back on his shoulders.

'Pray for me,' cried Atlas as Herakles left. 'Goodbye . . .'

Herakles would never forget the sad sight of Atlas, scorched by the fierce African sun, holding up the world for the rest of mankind.

By the time Herakles got back to King Eurystheus, he had only six months left to serve him.

'A quickie this time,' said the King. 'Go to the underworld and bring back Cerberus, the hound which guards the Gates of Hades.'

'Some quickie!' moaned Iolaus as they crossed the River Styx and entered the World of the Dead. Hades and Persephone were waiting for them.

'You may borrow Cerberus,' they said. 'On condition you catch him with your bare hands and you bring him back unharmed.'

'I'll do my best,' said Herakles, and strolling up to the three-headed Hound of Hell, he grabbed its huge head and squeezed it hard.

'Owwwww!' howled Cerberus and immediately fell to the ground.

'Take him to King Eurystheus – but bring him back soon,' said Persephone.

'Woof!' said Cerberus.

He was a good dog once they left the underworld, he walked to heel and didn't snap at anybody. In Mycenae he turned very nasty.

'WOOOF! WOOOF!' he snarled at weedy King Eurystheus. The King jumped on his throne.

'Praise be to Zeus, your labours are finished!' he shouted at Herakles. 'Now get out of here and never — *ever* — come back!'

'Wooof!' snapped Cerberus and bit the King's toe just as they were leaving.

'Good boy,' laughed Iolaus. 'I've been wanting to bite him for years!'

Herakles took Cerberus back to Hades, then he went home too, but after all his marvellous adventures, he couldn't settle to a quiet life. He wanted more adventures, so he travelled the world looking for them. Finally he became a god, not as great as his father Zeus, but a good god and a great hero — Herakles, the strongest man that ever lived!

7. Theseus and the Minotaur

When the great hero, Theseus, was born his father, Aegeus, did a very odd thing. He left him and went away to Athens where he became King.

'When my son grows up,' said Aegeus, 'give him these gifts.'

He ordered six of his soldiers to lift an enormous boulder and put a sword and a pair of sandals underneath it.

'That's not fair!' cried Theseus' mother. 'How will anybody be able to lift that boulder again?'

'My son will,' said Aegeus. 'Tell him to visit me in Athens, carrying the sword and wearing the sandals, then I will know who he is.'

With that he left and Theseus' mother never saw him again.

Aegeus was right about Theseus – the boy did grow up to be a-m-a-z-i-n-g-l-y strong. He could throw a discus, wrestle and run better than any other boy in the city. By the time he was a young man, Theseus was restless. He didn't want to stay at home with his mother, he wanted adventures.

'I must leave and visit my father in Athens,' he said one day.

'I know,' said his mother sadly. 'Take your

father's gifts with you.'

'Gifts, what gifts?' asked Theseus.

'I will show you,' said his mother.

She took Theseus to the boulder and pointed at it.

'Your father left them under there,' she said.

'Mother! Are you joking?' laughed Theseus.

'No. Your father said you would lift the boulder if you were his son.'

'Well, there's no doubt about that!' said Theseus.

He rubbed his hands, took a deep breath and grabbed hold of the enormous boulder.

'Ha-hhh!' he cried and lifted it.

Underneath were the sandals and the sword his father had left for him.

'Take them and wear them in Athens,' said his mother. 'Your father will know who you are and welcome you.'

Weeping, she kissed her son goodbye and prayed to the Gods to protect him.

When Theseus got to Athens, Medea the witch was waiting for him. She had told King Aegeus that the handsome stranger was an enemy soldier who would try to kill him.

'He must be destroyed!' she cried. 'Before he destroys you and your kingdom.'

'Yes!' cried Aegeus. 'I'll kill him with my own sword.'

'Leave the killing to me!' smiled Medea. 'Watch . . .' She mixed poison with wine and poured it into a beaker.

'This is for the stranger!' she cackled. 'Ha, ha, ha!'

When Theseus came to the palace, Medea gave him the drink.

'Welcome, stranger,' she smiled.

'Your health!' said Theseus, and he was just about to gulp back the poison when King Aegeus saw his sandals.

'NO-OOOO!' he yelled and smashed the beaker to the ground. 'Witch! This is my son, Theseus. You tried to kill him! Get out and never come back!'

'I put a curse on you, Aegeus!' she screamed.

'OUT!' yelled the King. 'Before I have you thrown out, in little pieces.'

Medea ran away to another country in the far north where luckily nobody has ever seen her since, but her curse stayed with Aegeus . . . as you will soon learn.

Theseus and the King were happy together, but only for a short time. Every nine years the King of Athens had to send seven of his strongest boys and seven of his loveliest girls to Crete, to King Minos, who forced them to dance before the giant bull, the Minotaur. It was a dance to the death, for no matter how quick and brave they were, the bull always killed the dancers, spearing them on his horns, then eating them, alive!

This bull was the same Cretan Bull that brave Herakles had captured years ago. It had escaped from Mycenae and returned to Crete, where King

Minos had asked his cleverest inventor to build a prison for it.

'Something really complicated, that nobody can get in or out of — especially the bull!'

Daedalus the inventor had thought about the problem for a long time and then come up with the brilliant idea of a maze.

'A maze,' he'd explained to the King. 'Circles within circles within circles, with the Minotaur in the middle.'

'Amazing! Ha, ha! That's a joke — a-mazing!' laughed King Minos.

Daedalus smiled politely — the King was famous for his rotten jokes. Anyway, he built the maze and put the bull in the middle, where it lived off human flesh, bull dancers, fed to it once a year.

When Theseus heard about the Minotaur he cried, *'I'll go!'*

'YOU!' exploded the King. 'You're my son, I won't let you be killed by a raging bull.'

'He won't kill me!' laughed Theseus. 'I'll kill him!'

He joined the girls and boys on the ship and the black sails were lifted.

'We'll be back!' called Theseus to the crowd waving them off at the harbour. 'And when we return, our sails will be white. Remember that, Father. If the Minotaur kills me, the sails will be black, but look for white — I'm going to sort out this Minotaur once and for all! Farewell!'

The ship lifted on the waves and sailed quickly

out of the harbour, its black sails gloomy against the sparkling blue sea. The girls and boys on board wept and wept, but Theseus promised he'd save all of them – or die trying!

When they reached Crete, Theseus went straight to the palace at Knossos and asked to speak to King Minos.

'I'm Theseus,' he said. 'I've come to kill the Minotaur!'

King Minos nearly fell off his throne, for never had so brave a hero stood before him. His beautiful daughter, Ariadne, immediately fell in love with the young man from Athens.

'I won't let this one be killed by the Minotaur,' she decided, and hurried off to talk to Daedalus, the inventor.

'I want you to help me save Theseus and the other Athenian boys and girls from the bull,' she said.

'No!' yelled Daedalus. 'Your father will kill me.'

'Please, please, please, p-l-e-a-s-e!' she begged.

'Oh, all right,' agreed Daedalus. 'But you must never tell anybody that I helped you – promise?'

'Promise!' said Ariadne.

'Theseus' life will depend on this!' He handed Ariadne a big ball of string. 'He must tie the end of the string to the gate at the start of the maze. The string will unroll as he walks along and will guide him back – if he's still alive!'

'That's brilliant!' cried Ariadne.

'To kill the Minotaur, Theseus must rip one of its horns from its head and stab the monster with it, right between the eyes.'

Ariadne went white as a sheet. 'That's impossible,' she gasped.

'Believe me, it's the only thing that will kill the bull,' said Daedalus. 'Now off you go, and don't tell a soul about our meeting.'

Ariadne hurried away and found Theseus. 'I will save you, hero, if you'll take me back to Athens and marry me,' she said.

'Yes!' said Theseus, who thought Ariadne was the loveliest woman he'd ever seen.

Ariadne smiled. 'This is what you must do . . .'

The next day Theseus went to the maze.

'Wait for me here,' he told the other boys and girls. 'If I'm not back in an hour, you're next.'

With tears in their eyes, they watched him disappear into the dark, winding circles of the labyrinth.

'Goodbye, Theseus,' they called. 'Good luck!'

With his sword raised, Theseus walked on . . . and on . . . and on! It got darker and spookier as he turned corner, after corner, after corner! Suddenly Theseus stopped dead in his tracks. He could hear a terrible, blood-chilling roaring.

'Zeus, ruler of the skies, help he,' he prayed.

Another noise burst through the labyrinth, a noise so loud it made his hair stand on end – the thundering of hoofs so big the ground trembled beneath his feet. Theseus turned his head this way and that, trying to guess which way the Minotaur would come at him. With a roar, it crashed through the centre of the maze and stood glaring at Theseus, its nostrils blazing fire, its head bent, horns gleaming white and sharp as razors.

Theseus stood and stood and stood, until he could feel the monster's blazing nostrils scorching his toes – then he jumped. With amazing strength and bravery, he leapt right between the Minotaur's horns and landed on its back. Theseus held on, balancing on the Minotaur's back like a dancer. The bull tossed its head, trying to throw him up and spear him on its huge horns, but Theseus held tighter and tighter and tighter. Suddenly he yanked one of the horns clean out of the bull's head, then leapt through the air and landed in front of the Minotaur.

'Dance with me!' he laughed.

Dripping blood, the crazy bull pawed the ground and then charged. It came at Theseus once more but he didn't move, he didn't even tremble. Lifting the horn like a javelin, he threw it with all his might. His aim was spot on. The horn hit the Minotaur right between the eyes and it fell to the ground, howling in pain. Grabbing the horn, Theseus ran back through the labyrinth, following the string's every twist and turn.

His friends couldn't believe their eyes when he burst out, his fist held high in victory.

'I killed it!' he cried. 'Now, let's get out of here!'

With the Cretan army chasing them like bloodhounds, Theseus and his friends raced to the

harbour where Ariadne was waiting for them on board ship.

'Set sail!' she yelled, and with the wind puffing out their black sails, they whisked across the dancing sea, singing and laughing.

'Hurray! Theseus has killed the Minotaur!'

Theseus was *so* happy he forgot all about the sails, so instead of changing them to white they stayed black. When his father saw them blowing against the blue sky, he cried out in agony.

'Ahhhh! My son is dead!'

Medea's wicked curse had come true. Aegeus threw himself off the cliffs, and from that day to this, the sea in which Aegeus drowned has been called the Aegean Sea, in memory of him.

Theseus' great journey had come to an end. He became a great king of Athens, but he never did marry the beautiful Ariadne. Dionysus, the God of Wine, took her away to live with him on Mount Olympus, and Theseus was wise enough to know that a mortal, even a great hero, never challenges the Gods!

8. Daedalus and Icarus

When the Minotaur was killed by Theseus, King Minos knew exactly who was to blame.

'Daedalus!' he yelled. 'You told Theseus the way out of the maze!'

'Not quite, Your Majesty. I told your daughter and *she* told him.'

'Hah!' shouted Minos, who would have liked to kill Daedalus right there and then, but he didn't. A live inventor is better than a dead one, especially when he's a brilliant one.

'You can live, but you're not going to enjoy yourself,' snapped Minos. 'I'm going to lock you in the maze and throw away the key.'

Daedalus, with all his tools and his workbench, was taken to the maze by soldiers.

'You won't get out of here in a hurry,' they laughed. 'Not unless you can fly!'

But the inventor had a plan of escape so brilliantly clever nobody could ever have guessed it.

'King Minos, before you lock me away, will you allow me one last favour?' he asked.

'What?' asked the King.

'Can my son, Icarus, come with me?'

'No!' answered the King. 'This isn't a party, this is prison.'

'But, Your Majesty, I can't work on my own. I need somebody to help me invent things, somebody young and strong, like my son,' coaxed Daedalus.

'Hum, all right then,' agreed the King. 'But he'd better work hard – you too!'

As soon as he was alone with his son, Daedalus grabbed hold of him and hugged him.

'Oh, Icarus!' he cried. 'We're going to get out of here, together!'

Icarus looked at the maze and the heavy metal gates blocking the entrance.

'Out!' he gasped. 'How?'

Daedalus smiled. 'We're going to fly,' he cried and started to run round the maze, flapping his arms and laughing. 'Wheeeee!'

Icarus thought his father had gone mad.

'Stop it, Father, we're not birds,' he said. 'How can you expect us to fly?'

'Because I'm going to make a flying machine,' answered Daedalus. 'And you're going to help me.'

In secret they set to work. To start with, they build a light, wooden frame.

'We'll strap it around us like this,' said Daedalus, fastening the frame on to his chest. 'And then we'll stick feathers on with wax.'

'Feathers?' cried Icarus. 'Where do we get feathers in this maze?'

'We get them from up there,' said Daedalus, nodding at two huge golden eagles circling the sky above the labyrinth. 'We shoot them.'

Luckily Icarus was a good shot with his catapult. He killed the birds which they then plucked.

'Now melt the wax,' said Daedalus. 'And dip each feather into the hot wax . . . like this.'

Icarus watched his father and did the same. They stuck all the feathers they'd plucked on to the frames and left them to dry for a week. Then they strapped their flying frames on to their chests and flapped their wings.

'How does it feel?' asked Daedalus.

'Wonderful!' smiled Icarus. 'Let's go right now, Father.'

'No, wait till morning,' said Daedalus. 'We'll leave at dawn, when the guards are sleepy.'

When the sun came up, Daedalus and his son strapped on their golden wings.

'Here we go!' cried Daedalus.

'One, two, three — and away!'

Up they went, high into the blue, blue sky.

'Look at me, Father!' shouted Icarus. 'I'm a bird — I can f-l-y!'

He was so excited he flew higher and faster than Daedalus, dipping and diving like a swallow.

'Be careful!' called his father. 'Don't go too near the sun or it will melt your wings.'

Icarus didn't hear him. 'Wheeee!' he cried as he zipped through a cloud and zoomed high into the sky. 'Father, you're a genius!'

As Icarus flew nearer and nearer to the sun, Daedalus could see the wax on his wings start to

bubble and boil.

'NO! NO!' screamed Daedalus. 'The sun!'

Too late. Icarus was falling, tumbling and turn-ing. He reached out his hands and cried for help. 'Father, save me!'

There wasn't a thing Daedalus could do. With a terrible cry, Icarus fell into the sea – the Icarian Sea, named in memory of him, the first boy ever to fly like a bird.

9. The Wooden Horse of Troy

The Trojan War began when Paris, Prince of Troy, fell madly in love with Helen, the most beautiful woman in the world.

'I'll marry her,' cried Paris, 'and make her my queen.'

'You can't do that,' said the Trojans. 'She's married to the King of Sparta.'

Paris wouldn't listen to any of them. He snatched Helen away from her husband and there was an almighty bust-up. Led by Agamemnon, the mighty warrior king of Mycenae, the Greeks declared war on the Trojans. Heroes from all over the land marched to join Agamemnon – Achilles, Odysseus, Ajax, Menelaus and Diomedes, they all came with their armies. When the battleships were ready, they set sail for Troy, the greatest army ever seen in Greece.

'Goodbye! Goodbye!' called their friends and family.

How could any of them have known that they would be away from home for ten long years?

When the Greeks landed on the shores of Troy, the Trojan army was lined up, waiting for them. Swords clashed, daggers slashed, clubs smashed,

men were killed by the thousand. Both sides knew that this, the first battle, would be an important one. Achilles fought like a devil. He aimed his spear at a tall Trojan warrior called Cycnus. The spear hit him full in the chest, but Cycnus didn't die, he didn't even bleed. Achilles thumped him and Cycnus didn't bat an eyelid. Achilles grabbed him tightly around the throat and squeezed the life out of him. Suddenly the strangest thing happened. A great white swan rose out of Cycnus' body. It flapped its wings and circled the sky above Achilles' head, then flew out across the sea where it settled on the waves.

'Who was this man?' asked Achilles.

'Cycnus, son of Poseidon, the Sea God,' answered the Trojans, and ran away frightened by what they had seen.

The Greeks were overjoyed that they'd won the first battle, but many, many more followed. Sometimes the Greeks won, sometimes the Trojans, but nobody would give in, especially Prince Paris who would not give up his beautiful Helen.

One, two, three, four, five, six, seven, eight, nine, ten long years passed and hundreds died on both sides. It wasn't as bad for the Trojans as it was for the Greeks, because they were inside their own city walls, near their family and friends. The Greeks were a long way from home, camped on the sea shore, boiling hot in the summer, freezing in the winter, and always, always starving hungry.

'We're sick and tired of this rotten war!' shouted the Greek soldiers. 'We want to go home!'

Agamemnon turned to Odysseus, King of Ithaca. 'You're the clever one – think of something,' he said.

Odysseus was a *very* clever man. He prayed to Athene, Goddess of Wisdom. 'Sweet Goddess, help me save the Greeks.'

Now up on Olympus, the Gods and Goddesses had been arguing for years about who should win the war.

'The Trojans, of course!' said Poseidon.

'The Greeks!' shouted Athene.

'Who cares?' yawned Zeus.

'I care!' cried Athene.

Wise Athene told Odysseus to build a huge wooden horse and pack it full of Greek soldiers. Odysseus couldn't believe his ears.

'Put my army in a wooden horse?' he gasped.

'Trust me, it will work,' said Athene.

When he told his men to build a giant wooden horse, they laughed themselves silly, but he ordered them to do it – or die. Half the army stayed with Odysseus and built the horse while the other half pretended to sail away.

'You must come back on the third night and meet me inside the city of Troy,' Odysseus told Agamemnon.

'INSIDE!' laughed Agamemnon.

'Trust me,' said Odysseus, remembering the words of the Goddess Athene. 'It will work.'

The Trojans couldn't believe their eyes when they saw the Greek ships sailing away.

'HURRAY! We've won!' they yelled. 'The Greeks are leaving. They've given up. HURRAY!'

For the first time in ten years, the Trojans flung open their city gates and ran outside. Then they saw the horse!

'Aaahhh! W-w-w-w-what's *that*?' they cried.

'It's a trick!' cried Paris. 'Quick, get back inside the walls.'

The Trojans hid behind their wall and watched the horse all day and all night . . . nothing happened. Priam and some of his men went out the next day and walked round the horse, tapping it.

'It's hollow,' said Priam. 'There's nothing inside it.'

Deep down inside the horse's belly, Odysseus smiled.

'Maybe it's a gift from the Gods,' said Priam.

'Yes!' cried the Trojans. 'The Gods are pleased we won the war and they've left this beautiful horse to prove it.'

'Quick, we'd better take it inside the city,' said Priam, 'or the Gods will be angry with us for not looking after their gift.'

They dragged the great wooden horse into Troy and that night they had an enormous party — even the guards at the gate joined in! Everybody got very drunk and they danced and sang till dawn, then they fell fast asleep. When all was quiet, Odysseus opened the secret trapdoor

underneath the horse's belly and his men crawled out. Eurylochus ran to open the city gates and Agamemnon marched in, followed by a thousand Greeks.

'CHARGE!'

The Greeks ran through the city, setting fire to everything and killing anybody who got in their way. The Trojans didn't stand a chance — the war was over. The Greeks had won, thanks to clever Odysseus.

'Let's go home!' cried Odysseus.

'Yes!!' shouted the Greeks.

Little did they know as they set off across the Aegean Sea, that another journey was only just starting!

10. Polyphemus, the Cyclops

Odysseus left Troy with his men, but it took them another ten years to get home. Poseidon, the Sea God, was especially angry with Odysseus. 'He's beaten the Trojans, AND burnt Troy to the ground,' he roared. 'You'll suffer, Greek!'

He whipped up the seas of the world and blew Odysseus' ship straight to the island of the Cyclopes, where his son, Polyphemus the one-eyed monster, lived.

'Kill the Greeks,' Poseidon said.

'No problem, Dad!' said Polyphemus. 'I'll kill them and eat them for tea!'

He wasn't joking either!

Odysseus and his men were half dead when their ship landed on the island. Tired and hungry, they searched around looking for food. When they found a cave full of sheep's milk and cheese, they all started to eat.

'No!' shouted Odysseus. 'That's bad manners. We must wait for the shepherd to come back and ask him for food.'

Suddenly hundreds of sheep ran into the cave. Then a massive shadow filled the cave as the Cyclops shuffled in and rolled a boulder over the

entrance. He stopped and sniffed the air, his single red eye whizzing and whirling in the middle of his head.

'I smell men!' he roared.

Terrified, the Greeks ran into the dark corners of the cave and hid, but the Cyclops found ten of them.

'Yum! Yum! Supper,' he slobbered and gobbled them down in a flash.

Odysseus was furious. 'Something's *got* to be done!' he said.

Stepping from the shadows, he held out his wineskin. 'Sir!' he called. 'Would you like a drink with your supper?'

'Drink?' roared the Cyclops.

'Yes, sir,' answered Odysseus. 'Good wine from Troy.'

'Wine! Mmmm, don't mind if I do,' said the Cyclops. 'It'll give me a good appetite. You're next on the menu, Greek!'

'Ha, ha!' laughed Odysseus. 'Very funny!'

'Cheers!' said the Cyclops and, snatching the wineskin, he knocked back the wine. GULP! GULP! GULP!

'Hic! That's delishush!' he burped. 'Have a drink with me, er . . . what's your name?'

'My name, sir, is Noname,' answered clever Odysseus.

'Noname, thash a funny name. Hic!'

'Here, have more, sir,' said Odysseus, handing him another wineskin.

'Don't mind if I do,' said the Cyclops, and he quickly emptied the second wineskin. 'Mmm, that's made me feel peckish.' He stared at Odysseus with his one red eye. 'Now I'll eat *you!*'

'First you've got to catch me, One-Eye!' laughed Odysseus, and he started to run circles round the Cyclops.

'Oooh! Don't do that,' said Polyphemus. 'It makes me feel dizzy.'

He tried to chase Odysseus, but he was too drunk to stand. He fell over and crashed to the floor, fast asleep. Odysseus grabbed a huge log and stuck it in the fire. When the end of the log was red-hot and as sharp as a pencil, he told his men to lift it out.'

'When I say three, shove it in the Cyclops' eye,' said Odysseus.

'Shove it in his eye!' cried the Greeks.

'One, two, three!' yelled Odysseus.

The Greeks ran straight at the sleeping Cyclops and plunged the red-hot log into his eye.

'AHHHHH!' screamed the Cyclops.

With blood pouring from his eye, he jumped to his feet and tried to hit the Greeks, but he couldn't see them. He scrambled around the cave on his hands and knees and then started to cry like a baby. 'Boo-hoo-hoo!'

'Baaa-aaa,' went his sheep.

'Oh, my little lambkins,' wept the Cyclops. 'Come to Daddy.'

The sheep skipped over to the Cyclops, who

rolled away the enormous boulder so that they could run outside and play in the meadow.

'Baaa-aaa!' went the sheep as they ran free.

'Quick,' said clever Odysseus. 'Grab a sheep's skin and cover yourselves.'

The Greeks watched Odysseus throw a sheep's fleece over his back, then fall down on to his hands and knees.

'Baaa!' bleated Odysseus and headed for the entrance of the cave.

The Greeks copied him. 'Baaaa! Baaa! Baaaa!' they went.

The Cyclops felt each of the men as they crept under his hands. 'BAA,' they bleated.

'Off you go,' he said, 'out into the meadows.'

One by one the Greeks ran free. The minute they were outside the cave, they threw off their sheep's skins and danced for joy.

'Fooled you, One-Eye!' yelled Odysseus. 'Baaaa!'

'Noname!' cried the Cyclops. 'You tricked me.'

'Tricked you easy, you great turnip head,' laughed Odysseus.

Polyphemus let out a great roar that shook the island. 'FRIENDS – HELP ME!' he bellowed.

Suddenly there was a noise like thunder as all the other Cyclopes on the island came running to help Polyphemus.

'Quick! Back to the ship!' cried Odysseus.

'I've been blinded!' wailed Polyphemus.

'Hah! Who did this terrible thing to you?' asked his friends.

'Noname,' answered Polyphemus.

'Noname!' cried the Cyclopes. 'What are you talking about?'

'The man who blinded me was called Noname,' said Polyphemus.

'Stop playing around!' snapped the angry Cyclopes. 'We've got better things to do than listen to this silly nonsense. Noname, indeed!'

In a bad temper they all stomped off. Old One-Eye was furious. He picked up boulders the size of a house and hurled them into the sea. The waves rose up and sent the ship spinning across the sea to Africa. The angry sea god Poseidon chased

them all the way there and all the way back again.

'I'll get you, Greek, for blinding my son!'

For ten long years Poseidon sent Odysseus and his men journeying across the world. They were old and tired by the time they got back to Ithaca, but nobody had forgotten the brave men who'd sailed away to Troy twenty years before. They were welcomed home like heroes, especially Odysseus, who was not only brave and strong, but brilliantly clever too.